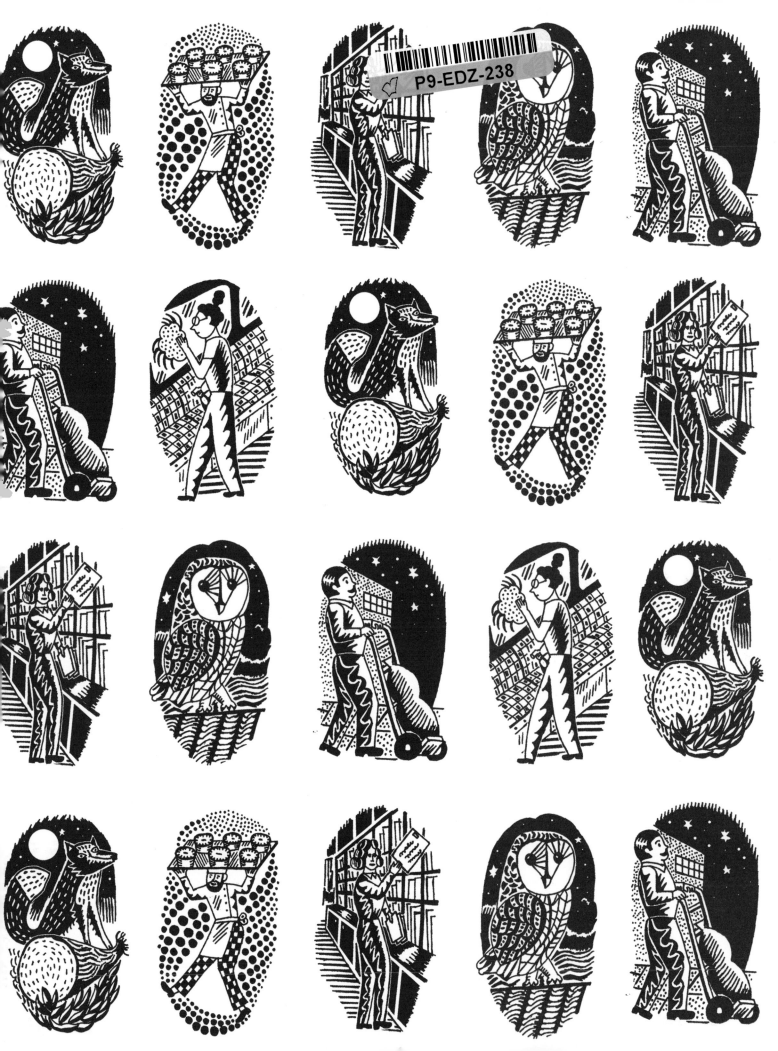

WHILE YOU'RE SLEEPING

First published in the UK in 2020 by
Pavilion Children's Books
43 Great Ormond Street
London, WC1N 3HZ
An imprint of Pavilion Books Company Limited

Text © Mick Jackson 2020
Illustrations © John Broadley 2020

The moral rights of the author and illustrator have been asserted

Publisher: Neil Dunnicliffe
Editor: Hattie Grylls
Designer: Sarah Crookes

ISBN: 9781843654650

A CIP catalogue record for this book is available from the British Library.

10 9 8 7 6 5 4 3 2 1

Reproduction by Mission, Hong Kong
Printed and bound by Toppan Leefung Ltd, China

This book can be ordered at www.pavilionbooks.com, or try your local bookshop.

WHILE YOU'RE SLEEPING

By Mick Jackson
& John Broadley

Oh, it's good to be snug,
deep under the covers,
good to slowly drift off to sleep.
But when you're all tucked up and dreaming
other people are wide-awake...

...busy cleaning the trains
and buses you rode on
just a few hours earlier.

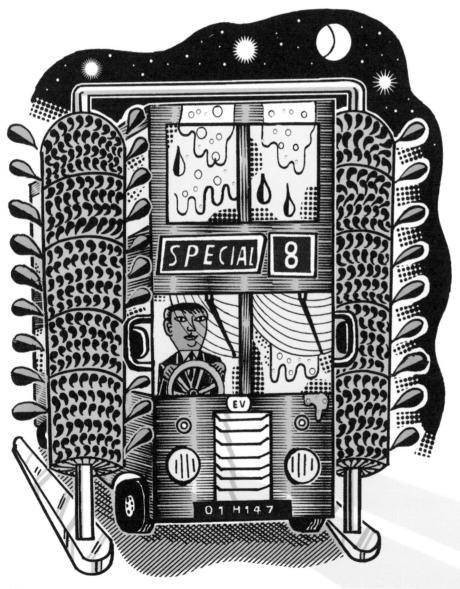

Cleaning the streets
and shops and offices.

Oh, there's plenty needs doing
at night time.
There's plenty going on.

Think of all those letters and packages
being sorted into counties... towns... and streets.
Bagged-up and handed to postmen and women –
a birthday present, perhaps,
slowly heading towards your house.

Bakers wake in the dark
and turn on their enormous ovens
to bake their cakes and loaves and pies.

Some shops stay open
right through the night.

You can buy anything you need there
whenever you need it.

At the fire station firefighters sit
and read a book or listen to the radio,
waiting for the call to come.
Then, when the big bell rings they jump up,
slide down the pole,
climb into their fire engines
and head off down the dark, dark streets.

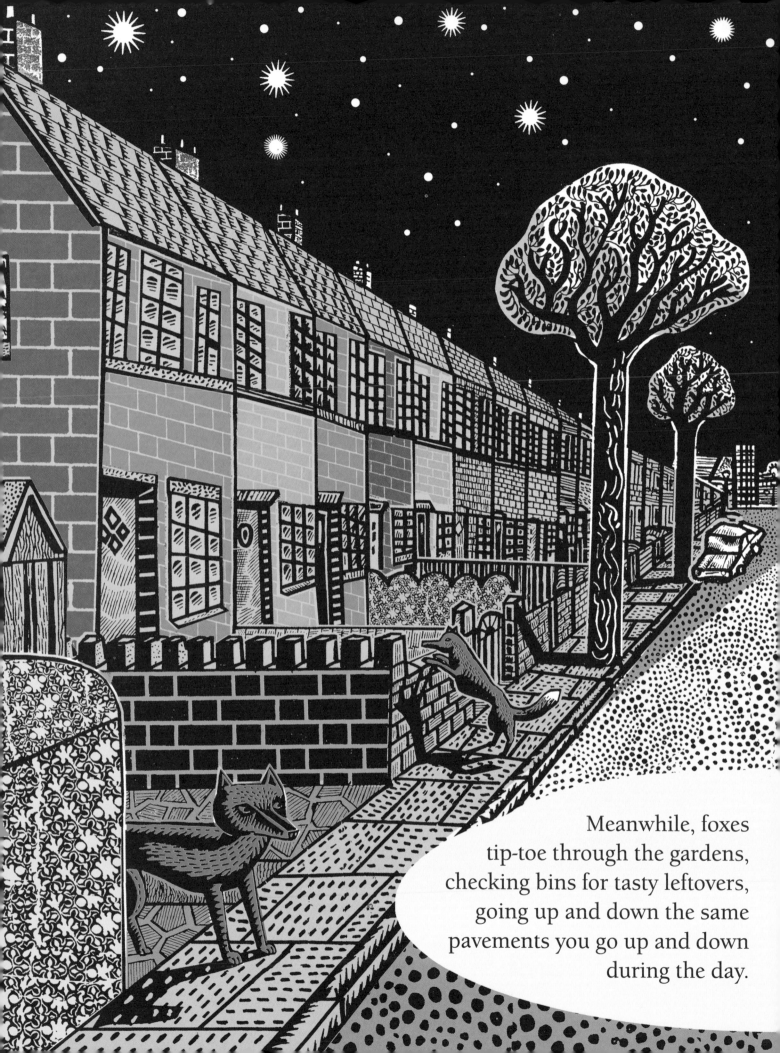

Meanwhile, foxes tip-toe through the gardens, checking bins for tasty leftovers, going up and down the same pavements you go up and down during the day.

Sometimes a
night-worker and a
fox will pass by each other...
nod to one another,
then carry
on their way.

Hospitals keep busy
right through the night,
like little cities.
People having their babies,
people being cared for.

Some sleeping,
some still awake.

And in every town some mum or dad will be up with their little ones,
sitting in a tiny pool of light.
Young babies need changing and feeding every two or three hours.
It can take a while for them to learn to sleep right through.

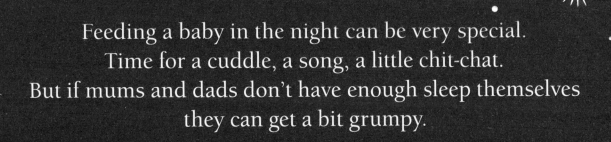

Feeding a baby in the night can be very special.
Time for a cuddle, a song, a little chit-chat.
But if mums and dads don't have enough sleep themselves
they can get a bit grumpy.

Then they're not much fun to be around.

Out of town,
an owl sweeps across a field...
bats fly low over lakes and hedges...
hungry hares look for food.

Sometimes at night
the rain falls
on the hills and valleys...

And out at sea ships cut through the waves
on their week-long voyages,
boats slowly make their way back to land.
Above them, a million stars look down.
The mighty wind helps them on their way.

Sometimes you'll wake, deep in the night
– a bad dream, maybe...

...or something else
that's not quite
right –

and no matter how hard you try
sleep simply will not come.

Then, just think of all the
people hard at work,
think of the night-time animals,

the fire station
and hospital,

the shops,

the all-night cafés.

Or think how
at that very moment
somewhere else in the world
another boy or girl is
sitting in class...
watching TV...

sledging...
or swimming in the sea.

Maybe that will help.

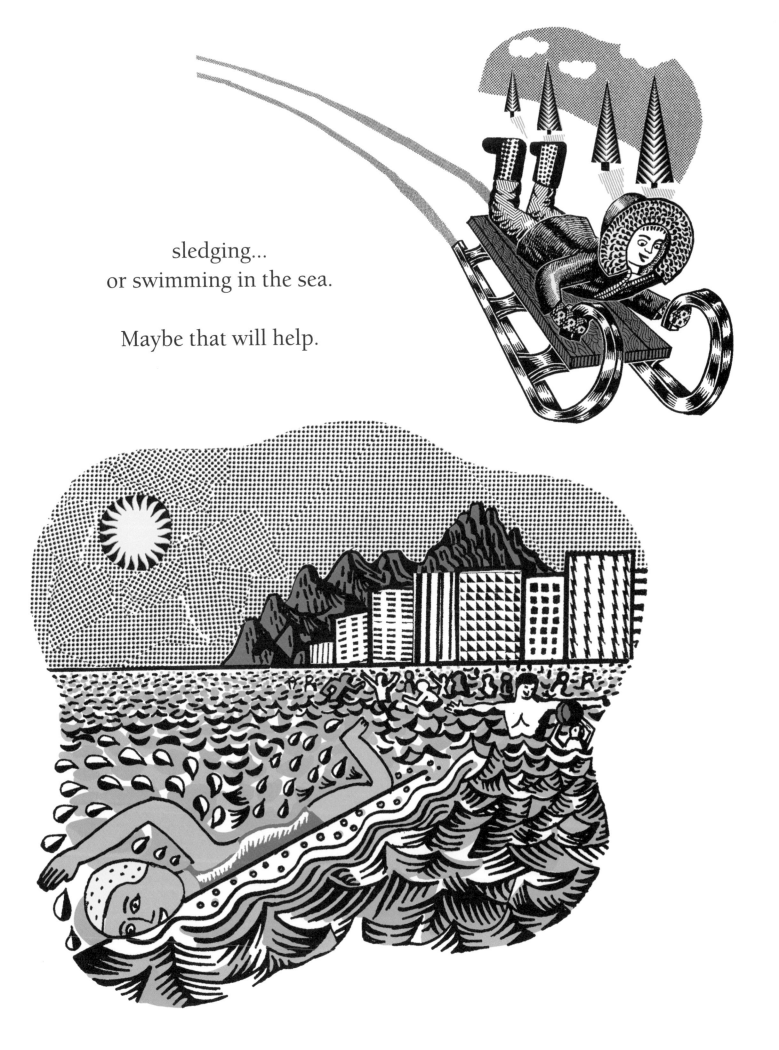

And when you wake in the morning,
think of all those night-time workers
arriving home, slow and exhausted.
Climbing the stairs, cleaning their teeth
and sliding under the covers...

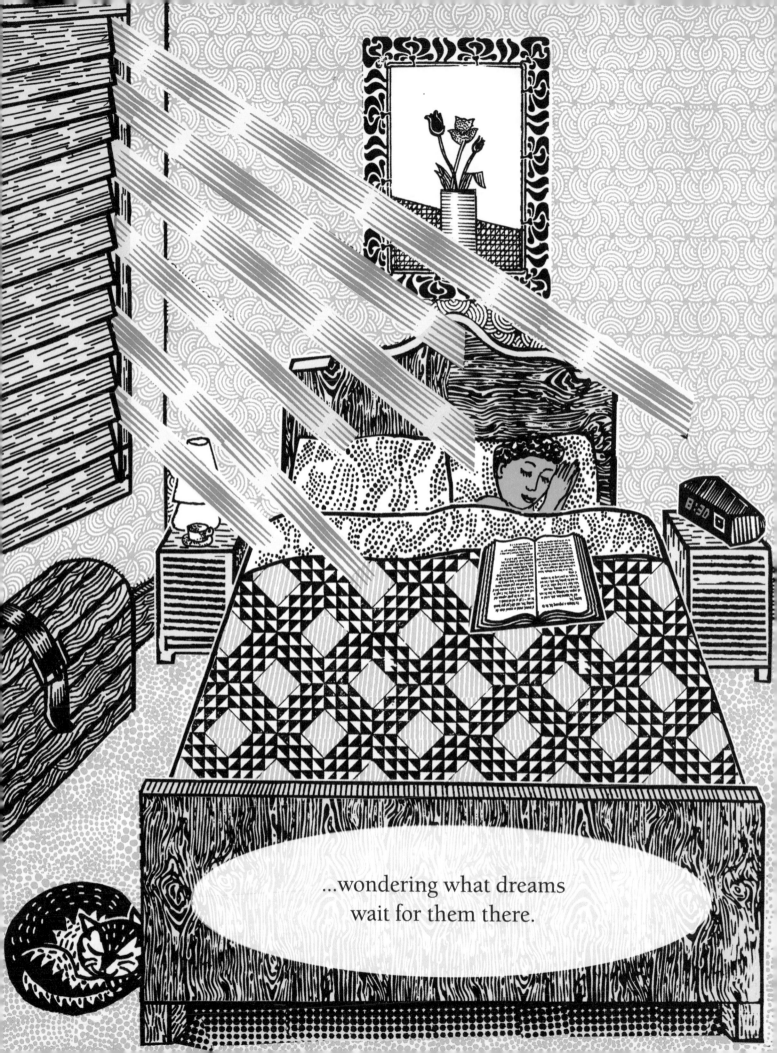

...wondering what dreams
wait for them there.